Air Man

Air Man was the scariest-looking robot that Mega Man had ever seen. He was big and he was strong, but the scary thing about him was his mouth.

Air Man's mouth was a huge, gaping hole that took in air and then blew it out in terrible gusts. Even though he was a robot, his body seemed like it was made out of clouds. As he moved, wisps of fog drifted off his pointed shoulders. Miniature tornadoes flew from his mouth, pointing their tails straight at Mega Man.

Air Man stood with his back against a wall, spitting out hundreds of tornadoes.

"Destroying you will be a breeze, Mega Man!" he shouted.

MEGA MAN 2®

A novel based on the best-selling game
by CAPCOM®

Book created by F.X. Nine
Written by Ellen Miles
A Seth Godin Production

**This book is not authorized, sponsored, or endorsed
by Nintendo of America Inc.**

SCHOLASTIC INC.
New York Toronto London Auckland Sydney

This book is dedicated to Jerry —
the original Mega Man

Special thanks to: Greg Holch, Jean Feiwel, Dick
Krinsley, Dona Smith, Eric Leinwand, Amy Berkower,
Sheila Callahan, Nancy Smith, Joan Giurdanella, and
especially Joe Morici, Chris Riggs and Kevin Sullivan.

ISBN 0-590-43772-0

12 11 10 9 8 7 6 5 4 3 2 1   0 1 2 3/9

Printed in the U.S.A.   40

First Scholastic printing, September 1990

CHAPTER ONE

"Welcome, welcome," said Dr. Light, smiling as he opened the door for Mega Man.

The lab looked pretty much the same as it always had. Beakers bubbled over as they boiled away on flaming burners. Bubbles rose through clear pipes, pushing red, yellow, and green liquids through a network of crazy plumbing.

Huge machines covered with lights pulsed and beeped as information sped through their circuits. Reams of paper were being spewed out, each page covered with numbers, letters, graphs, and formulas. Dr. Light was always working on a hundred different things at once.

"Mega Man," said Dr. Light. "I hate to have to tell you this news, but — "

"I know, I know," said Mega Man. "I saw it on the news-beam. Doctor Wily is back. I thought we had destroyed him, but I guess he's even stronger than we had imagined."

Dr. Light nodded. "And this time he's created eight of the most terrible robots ever built. Anyone who wants to capture Doctor Wiley has to get past each of those robots first." He looked at Mega Man. "You have fought many battles, Mega Man, and you have won them all. You may be invincible. You are the finest superrobot I have ever built."

Mega Man would have blushed if his circuits had been programmed for that activity.

"But I don't know if you would be able to fight your way to Doctor Wily alone," continued the doctor. "From what I understand, these robots are capable of the highest level of fighting ever imagined. And even if you do make it past them, you still have to fight your way into Doctor Wily's castle, and who knows what creatures he's created to protect him there!"

Mega Man nodded. He didn't look afraid. As he waited to hear what Dr. Light would say next, he thought about the past.

A few hours earlier he had been back in his comfortable little home sweet home, in the tiny village nestled high in a mountain valley. He had been watching the news-beam when his permanently attached proton beeper had gone off.

Its red light flashed as it beeped. That meant that Dr. Light was trying to reach him! Mega Man had tuned in the Doctor on his video screen.

"Mega Man, please report at once to my laboratory!" Dr. Light had said urgently.

Mega Man had looked around at his comfortable home and paused for a moment. There was no choice. He was a robot. He had to obey his creator.

Dr. Light was just as smart as Dr. Wily, but he

used his genius for good, not for evil. He had vowed long ago to do everything in his power to protect the universe from destruction. Dr. Wily had become his main enemy.

When Dr. Light first created Mega Man, he hadn't intended to make a superhero. Mega Man was originally created as a tool-using robot. He was small, but he was the best tool-using robot ever made.

He would be able to fix anything, using any kind of tool ever invented. He was programmed so that any tool put into his hands would automatically be used in the most effective and efficient way possible.

But soon after Mega Man was built, Dr. Light began to fear for the universe. Much evil was at work, all stemming from the mind of the fiendish Dr. Wily. Quickly, Dr. Light made some changes in his robot.

First, he programmed him to think of nothing but pure good, to seek out evildoers and to always fight on the side of truth and justice. Next, he upgraded Mega Man's tool-using capabilities to include all existing — and all imaginable — weapons.

Mega Man, the superrobot, had been created.

And what a robot he was. He'd fought every villain he'd come up against, fought them all to the finish. Or so he'd thought.

Now it looked like Dr. Wily had come back to

life, and this time he was more evil than ever.

Mega Man turned his attention back to Dr. Light.

"And so, Mega Man," said the doctor, "I have decided to clone you. To copy your circuits and create another Mega Man. Two of you together ought to be able to get the job done."

Mega Man nodded. He wasn't sure if this idea would work, but he was a robot. He had to obey his creator. "Okay, Doctor Light," he said. "How do we do it?"

Dr. Light gestured toward the back of the laboratory. Mega man saw a huge, freestanding box with open doors. A control panel on its side was blinking madly, flashing red and yellow lights.

"My latest invention," he said proudly. "The Robo-Transometer XZ-4000, with Cloning Capability." He led Mega Man to the door. "Please step inside," he said. "This won't hurt a bit. And when I open the door, there'll be two of you."

Mega Man walked into the box, and Dr. Light shut the door behind him. It was dark in there. And then the box began to shake. Mega Man reached out and tried to hold onto the walls as the quaking increased.

Then there was a series of loud booming sounds, followed by a crash of metal on metal. Something screeched, and a bell rang. Sirens sounded, whooping wildly in the total darkness. Mega Man fell to the shaking floor and was still.

4

CHAPTER TWO

The door of the Robo-Transometer swung open, letting in a stream of light. Mega Man stirred. His head hurt.

"My head hurts," he said.

"What?" shouted Dr. Light. "You're a robot! You're impervious to pain." Dr. Light charged past Mega Man and searched the interior of the box. "And why is there still only one of you?"

"I don't know," answered Mega Man. "But my head really does hurt."

Dr. Light approached Mega Man and examined his forehead. "No wonder it hurts," he said. "You've got a nasty bruise."

Then his mouth fell open. "A bruise?" Dr. Light looked puzzled. "Robots don't bruise! What have I done?" He thought for a moment and then pinched Mega Man on the arm, hard.

"Ouch!" yelled Mega Man. "Why did you do that?"

"I was checking something, and I think I've found the answer," said Dr. Light. "Come with me." He led Mega Man to another machine and hooked him up to it by attaching electrodes to Mega Man's neck. He watched the monitor closely as it blinked and flashed, showing formula after formula on the screen.

Then the monitor went blank for a moment. When it came back on, spelled out across the face of the screen were the words POSITIVE IDENTIFICATION CONFIRMED. SUBJECT IS HUMAN.

Mega Man blinked and looked again. He couldn't believe it. He wasn't a robot anymore. He was alive. Dr. Light turned to him and smiled. "How does it feel, Mega Man?" he asked.

Mega Man couldn't answer. He was still in shock.

"It was a mistake, I admit it. I must have just pushed the wrong sequence of buttons. But I think it will work out anyway," said Dr. Light. "According to the printout here, you have retained your full robot memory and will be able to function just as well as you always have in battle."

"B...but..." Mega Man stumbled over the words. "Am I still invincible?"

Dr. Light paused. His smile faded. "I don't know. I certainly hope so, but there's no way to be sure." He put his hand on Mega Man's shoulder. "You'll just have to be extra careful."

Mega Man felt something he'd never felt before. It was a strange feeling and it made him jumpy. The feeling was fear. It was a feeling he'd have to put behind him if he hoped to destroy Dr. Wily.

He gathered himself together and faced Dr. Light straight on. "I'm ready for my mission," he said. "Do you have a briefing for me on my robot enemies?"

Dr. Light looked down at Mega Man. He paused.

"I know what you're thinking," said Mega Man. "You think now that I'm human my size might work against me. You think I'm too small to do the job!" Dr. Light shook his head. "I might have thought that for a moment, but I have confidence in you," he said. "You may be small, but you're tough and you're determined. Step into my office and I'll tell you everything I know about Doctor Wily's robots."

Mega Man followed Dr. Light into his office and listened intently while the man explained how to fight each of the robots.

"Mega Man, in order to reach Doctor Wily, you'll have to destroy his eight robot guardians: Metal Man, Flash Man, Bubble Man, Air Man, Crash Man, Heat Man, Wood Man, and Quick Man. Each robot lives in a different weird world — and some of the robots have henchmen to do their dirty work. You'll have to battle them as well."

"I'll still be in contact with you through your proton-beeper," finished Dr. Light. "I'll be following all your activities. And when you're ready to leave one robot's empire and enter another, I'll give you the password."

"Okay, then Doctor Light," said Mega Man. "I'm off. It sounds as if I should start with Metal Man." He shook the doctor's hand. "Wish me luck!"

CHAPTER THREE

Crash! Boom! BangbangbangBANG! The noise was so loud that Mega Man could barely hear himself think. He looked around.

So this was Metal Man's world. Everywhere he looked, Mega Man saw machinery working. And all the machinery was *loud*.

Pistons pumped, coils uncoiled and springs sprung. Cogs turned and wheels revolved. And then there were the gears. Hundreds of them — no, thousands, as far as Mega Man could see.

Giant gears with teeth the size of refrigerators. The gears gnashed their teeth together, grinding with a noise louder than the loudest chain saw.

Mega Man winced. His ears hurt terribly, which was a new feeling for him. He wanted to put his hands over them to protect them from the noise, but he knew he had to be ready to defend himself. And how could he fire his Mega Gun with his hands over his ears?

Mega Man shook his head and tried to ignore the noise. He must move on — he must seek out and destroy Metal Man. That was his mission. That was why he was here.

He started to walk, balancing along the top of

a huge machine that pumped out steel parts. *Crash! Crash!* Mega Man wasn't doing very well at tuning out the noise.

Then he looked up and saw something that made him forget the din completely.

There was a huge iron weight dropping down onto him, fast! It looked like it weighed at least three tons. And the bottom, the part that Mega Man was looking up at, was covered with giant spikes.

Mega Man jumped and ran ahead as fast as he could. The weight crashed down behind him. He sighed with relief.

And then he heard another crash, right next to him. Another weight! And then another, and another. They were coming down all around him.

"This must be Dr. Wily's doing," said Mega Man, as he dodged the weights. "Well, he won't get *me* so easily!" He ran even faster, turning almost invisible as he zipped between the weights.

Then he spied a conveyor belt, rolling along between the clamorous machines. He jumped onto it. He needed a rest.

The belt carried him along, past huge machines that set off sparks as they pounded metal into new shapes.

The noise was overwhelming. As soon as he felt refreshed, Mega Man jumped off the conveyor belt and started to run through the maze of machinery. The belt just wasn't fast enough. He wanted to find Metal Man.

Mega Man ran fast, his head down. Suddenly, he crashed into a pile of barrels. He leapt over them and kept on running. Another pile of barrels tripped him up. Picking himself up, he realized that he'd better watch where he was going.

He kept moving quickly, but he kept an eye out for more barrels. He found that he could dodge most of them, and the rest he destroyed with his Mega Gun.

The noise was getting louder. It was thunderous. It was deafening. Then Mega Man saw a huge tower with a big W on it. Dr. Light had told him to watch for the tower. The W stood for Wily. Mega Man knew he must be getting closer to Metal Man's secret lair, in the center of his empire.

Sure enough, Mega Man soon came up against a huge iron door. He just knew that Metal Man must be behind it. He pounded on it with his fists, but it wouldn't budge. He kicked it as hard as he could, but it just stayed shut. Finally, he pulled out his Mega Gun and took aim at the lock.

He fired, and the door swung open. Mega Man entered, and the door slammed shut behind him with a huge crash. He walked a few feet only to find himself in front of another huge door. This time he didn't even pause. He fired away at the lock, ran in, and let the door slam behind him.

He looked to his right and to his left. This must be Metal Man's lair. But where was the evil robot? He heard a noise behind him and whirled around.

"Eat steel, 'Mini' Man,'" sneered the crafty robot. Metal Man was about as tall as Mega Man, but he was wrapped in shiny stainless steel. Every corner of his armor gleamed. Wrapped around his head was a garland of sharp steel spikes.

Mega Man ducked as Metal Man fired whirling steel blades at him. The blades cut through the air with the sound of cold metal. Mega Man aimed his Mega Gun and fired back. The shots just grazed the awesome metal-plated body of the evil robot.

Metal Man hurled more blades, but this time Mega Man jumped to avoid them, and fired back while he was still hovering in the air. *Pow!* A hit! Metal Man staggered, then regained his balance.

But before the robot could shoot more blades, Mega Man fired again, jumped over him, and fired once more. *Pow! Blam!* Metal Man exploded into a million gears, cogs, and flywheels.

Mega Man just stood there and grinned. "I always knew you were nothing but a heap of junk, Metal Man!" he said with a smile. He grabbed the Metal Blade, Metal Man's weapon, from where it lay on the ground.

Then he beeped Dr. Light. He was ready to move on to the next robot empire.

CHAPTER FOUR

Mega Man heard Dr. Light over the radio that was built into his helmet. Dr. Light was cheering. "All right, Mega Man! Good work," he said. "I watched the whole thing on my monitor."

"And now you've got the Metal Blade," he went on. "Terrific! That's a precious weapon: It's the only one that will have any effect on some of Doctor Wily's robots."

"Where to next, Doctor Light?" asked Mega Man.

"There's no question about it," said the doctor. "I'm going to key in the password for Flash Man's empire. Ready? "

Mega Man nodded.

"Good luck, then — here you go!" The doctor's voice faded out.

Mega Man looked around. Flash Man's empire was not a pleasant place. It was cold — a damp kind of cold — and gloomy. A dim blue light washed over his surroundings.

Mega Man saw that he was in the midst of a

group of old, ruined buildings. He would have to find his way through them, but the going would be treacherous. Loose bricks lay every which way, and tall towers looked like they were about to topple.

Mega Man checked his energy level. Dr. Light had supplied him with energy pellets, the same kind he'd taken when he was a robot. Dr. Light had told him to be sure to keep his energy high.

He took two pellets, since his reading was a little low. Then he checked his weapons and started out.

It was a relief to be out of the banging, clashing world of Metal Man. But Flash Man's world was just a little *too* quiet. Mega Man listened hard. He couldn't hear a thing. There was total silence.

Suddenly, a loud stomping noise shattered the quiet. Mega Man looked around wildly. Where was the noise coming from? He couldn't see a thing.

Then he looked up, just in time to see a giant foot about to smash down on top of him.

Mega Man put on a burst of speed and ran out from under the robot's foot. When he'd gone a safe distance, he turned to look back.

This was the most gigantic robot Mega Man had ever seen! It was ten times his size, towering high above him on massive legs. Its feet were the size of a small car, and its legs were like silos. "That must be Mr. Big," said Mega Man. "Doctor Light warned me about him. He's one of Flash Man's helpers."

Stomp! Stomp! Mr. Big kept on coming straight at Mega Man.

"Prepare to be flattened!" he roared.

Mega Man looked around desperately. The robot was coming toward him so fast that he didn't even have a chance to fire.

Then he spotted a tiny crack in the broken-down brick wall behind him. "Aha!" he said. "This is one time I'm happy to be as little as I am." The huge robot reached out to grab him, but Mega Man jumped into the crack just in time.

Mr. Big stopped and looked around. The giant robot was confused. Mega Man figured he must have looked as tiny as a mouse to the robot. And now he was just like a little mouse who had disappeared into his hole.

Mr. Big shrugged and stomped off in the other direction. Mega Man took a moment to check his weapons' energy levels and gear them up. Then he took off after the robot, leaping from brick to brick between the big buildings.

Mega Man moved quietly, sneaking up on the stomping robot from behind. When he had a clear shot, he fired the Metal Blade.

A hit! Mr. Big roared.

Mega Man fired again. The robot tried to turn and come after Mega Man, but his main circuits had been damaged.

Mega Man fired one more time, and this time Mr. Big fell down and didn't move again. The blades fired from the Metal Blade had cut through the robot's giant legs as if they were butter.

Mega Man looked at the fallen robot. "You may be big," he said. "But you know what they say! The bigger they are, the harder they fall."

Mega Man knew he had to keep moving. He had to find Flash Man.

He ran past the robot's fallen body and spotted an elevator moving up the wall of one of the tallest buildings. "This'll make my trip much faster," he said, hopping on.

He rode the elevator to the very top, hopped off, and ran through the building. At the end of a hallway he spotted an Energy Barrel. It was marked with a big E on its side.

Dr. Light had told him that he would see these along the way. Each barrel contained nutrients and vitamins — the same kind of quick energy that was in his energy pellets. As long as he kept finding barrels, he could keep his energy level up. Mega Man grabbed the barrel and powered up. Then he kept on running.

Suddenly, the air in front of him was filled with flying Boomeroids, little boomerang shaped robots that Dr. Light had told him to watch out for. They seemed to be self-propelled! Mega Man ducked and dodged, firing back with the Metal Blade.

What a great weapon! The Boomeroids blew into tiny pieces as the Metal Blade's flying blades cut them down.

Mega Man looked up ahead. There was a giant tower with the big W. He knew he was almost there.

Mega Man came to an iron gate. He used his superstrength to lift it, and it rolled up and then slammed back down once he was through. Another gate blocked his path, but it didn't even slow Mega Man down.

Suddenly, Flash Man appeared in front of him, dashing around and firing rapidly. Mega Man had never seen anything move so fast! And each time Flash Man fired, something strange happened. As each shot left Flash Man's weapon, Mega Man found that he was momentarily frozen in his tracks.

But Mega Man activated the autofire mechanism in the Metal Blade to fire again and again at his enemy.

And then it was over. Flash Man was destroyed. "You've got to be more than just a flash in the pan to beat me!" said Mega Man, smiling.

GAME HINT

To kill Air Man, carefully jump the tornadoes to get close to him.

CHAPTER FIVE

"Two down, six to go!" said Mega Man into his radio.

"That's right, Mega Man," answered Dr. Light. "But please be more careful. I thought you were done for when Mr. Big attacked."

"He just talks big. And Flash Man was no problem. These superrobots of Doctor Wily's aren't so tough if you know how to fight them," said Mega Man, boasting a little.

"Did you get Flash Man's Time Stopper?" asked Dr. Light. "What a weapon! It just freezes your enemies in place."

"Got it!" answered Mega Man, holding it up so that Dr. Light could see it over his monitor.

"Good!" said Dr. Light. "You'll need it." He paused for a moment, checking over his notes. "It looks like your next battle will be with Bubble Man. Get equipped with all your weapons. Ready for the password?"

"Ready!" Mega Man answered. And then Dr. Light's voice was gone. Static was all Mega Man could hear over his radio.

Mega Man looked down. He was hovering over water! There was water everywhere, as far as he could see. Frantic, he kicked with his feet and waved his arms, moving through the air until he was over a wooden pier.

He landed running. He was going to have to keep his wits about him in Bubble Man's world!

The water lapped against the pier he was running on. Mega Man wasn't ready to start swimming, not yet. But suddenly, he ran out of pier!

Mega Man leapt off the end of that pier and jumped onto the next one. He kept on running. Then, up ahead, he saw a giant frog! It was huge, and green, and very mean looking. That must be Croaker. Doctor Light had warned him about the robot henchmen he'd find. This was one of Bubble Man's fiendish helpers. Mega Man tried to run past Croaker.

Just then, Croaker opened his mouth. *"Ribbit! Ribbit!"* he croaked.

"That's the loudest frog I ever heard," said Mega Man. Then he noticed something. Every time Croaker said ribbit, five *little* Croakers jumped out of his mouth. And the little Croakers headed straight for Mega Man.

He was surrounded!

Mega Man grabbed his Mega Gun and fired away. It had no effect! Neither did the Time Stopper. These Croakers must be immune.

"Try ignoring this!" Mega Man said, firing the Metal Blade. Blades flew in every direction. Each shot destroyed at least three of the miniature Croakers. Mega Man kept firing until he had gotten past Croaker safely.

Finally, he was out of range. Mega Man was running hard, looking back over his shoulder to make sure that Croaker wasn't following him.

Suddenly, he tripped off the end of the pier he was running on and fell, head over heels, right into the water.

CHAPTER SIX

Mega Man fell through the water, drifting deeper and deeper. This was awful! He didn't even know if he'd be able to swim. As a robot he'd been a terrific swimmer, but would he still know how, now that he was human?

He tried a few underwater strokes and discovered that he could swim as well as he ever had. His helmet kept the water out. "Phew!" he said. "Lucky for me!"

And then, up ahead, Mega Man saw three Crabbots. These tiny robots looked like ugly crabs. They rode along on little wheels, their shells protecting them as they fired at the superhero.

Mega Man fired back with the Metal Blade. It was the only weapon he had that seemed to work underwater.

The shell flew off the first Crabbot, revealing the wheels below. Mega Man fired again until even the wheels were destroyed.

Then he aimed and fired, again and again, until he had taken care of all the other Crabbots.

Mega Man was swimming backward as he fired, so he didn't see the huge funnel until he'd fallen into it. He was sucked down into a pipe so fast that he could barely catch his breath.

Mega Man took a wild ride through a whole network of pipes. First he was upside down, then he was downside up. He was whirled around so much that soon he didn't know where he was.

Then the pipe spit him out as suddenly as it had sucked him in. Mega Man was very dizzy. He looked around, trying to get his bearings.

Which way was Bubble Man? Mega Man couldn't wait to get out of this superrobot's wet, wet world.

He started to swim again, hoping he was going in the right direction. Then he saw a huge tower ahead, with a big initial W. Below the tower were the gates to Bubble Man's lair.

Mega Man swam through the gates. Bubble Man was waiting for him. "Mega *blorble* man!" he cried. "How *gurgle* dare you enter my king-*burrrble*-dom!" Bubble Man's armor was green, and he had webbed hands and webbed feet, just like a frog. He wore a special helmet that looked like a scuba mask.

He fired his Bubble Lead straight at Mega Man. A huge bubble of molten lead rolled at him. Mega Man jumped and dodged. It was hard to move quickly underwater.

Mega Man aimed his Metal Blade and fired. Bubble Man slid to the left and dodged the flying blade.

Bubble Man laughed. "You'll never *blurble* get me, Mega Man!" he said. He fired his Bubble Lead again. A tiny bubble flew out, growing as it moved through the water. It got bigger and bigger as it came toward Mega Man.

This time Mega Man couldn't move quickly enough to dodge it. The now huge, heavy bubble rolled right over him, squashing him flat and knocking all the air out of him.

Mega Man lay still.

Bubble Man gloated. "Got you, Mega Man!" he laughed. "Doctor Wily *blorble* will be proud of me!"

Then there was a faint beeping inside Mega Man's helmet. Dr. Light's voice came through.

"Mega Man! Mega Man!" the doctor yelled. "Come in, Mega Man!" Dr. Light sounded frantic.

Mega Man blinked.

"I knew you weren't dead!" said Dr. Light. But he didn't sound so sure. "Now! Take an energy pellet and get your Metal Blade ready!"

The energy pellet took effect at once. Mega Man burst into action. He aimed the Metal Blade straight at Bubble Man and fired over and over.

Bubble Man tried to get out of range, climbing the giant net that decorated his lair, but it was too late.

Mega Man couldn't be stopped. Within seconds, Bubble Man had been destroyed.

Mega Man picked up the Bubble Lead. He beeped for Dr. Light. "Doctor Light!" he said, when his radio lit up. "Thanks! I thought it was all over for me."

"Oh, you would have been fine," said Dr. Light. "But I'm glad I could help out. Now, are you ready to take on your next villain?"

Mega Man felt full of energy. Finishing off Bubble Man had made him feel invincible. "Sure!" he said.

"All right," said Dr. Light. "It's time to meet Air Man."

GAME HINT

Use the Jet-Ski to get over the lava

CHAPTER SEVEN

Mega Man couldn't see a thing. He was surrounded by a damp, misty white fog. He beeped for Dr. Light. "Where am I, Doctor Light?" he asked.

But the doctor didn't answer. There was just a lot of static coming over the radio. Then, Mega Man heard what sounded like a weather report. He listened hard.

When it was over, Mega Man thought for a moment. "Hmmm...high winds? Gales? Hurricanes likely? Tornado warnings for all areas? Sounds like stormy weather ahead!"

Then he knew where he was. He was in Air Man's empire, and he was standing in the middle of a cloud. He started to run, following a pathway that appeared beneath his feet.

Finally, he found his way out of the cloud and into a blue, blue sky with plenty of other fluffy white clouds everywhere. It was beautiful, but Mega Man felt a shiver of fear. He wasn't used to being so high up.

Suddenly, his walkway ended. Mega Man looked around. Everywhere he looked he saw blue,

blue sky and puffy white clouds. Everywhere, that is, except straight ahead of him.

Straight ahead of him was a Cloud Climber. What a strange creature. Its huge red face frowned at Mega Man. Spikes grew out of the top of its flat head, then disappeared, then grew again.

Mega Man knew there was only one way for him to go. He'd have to jump right onto the floating Cloud Climber and use it as a stepping-stone.

He watched and waited until the spikes weren't in his way. Then he jumped and ran across the flat top of the Cloud Climber. The Cloud Climber was furious.

The frown on its face turned into a scowl, and miniature Cloud Climbers began to pop out of its ears. They swarmed over to Mega Man, surrounding him. Mega Man felt trapped. He had nowhere to run! There was only one thing to do. He'd have to fight them off.

Blam! Pow! Mega Man fired. The miniature Cloud Climbers turned into puffs of smoke. Mega Man breathed a sigh of relief.

He couldn't stop to rest, though. He had to keep moving if he was going to find Air Man. Mega Man jumped quickly to another large Cloud Climber, running fast, and then to another. Mega Man was on his way.

Then Mega Man heard a loud chop-chop-chopping noise. He looked up. Above him was a Roto-Chimp. What a strange creature! Half monkey, half helicopter. It rode through the air on a Thunder Chariot, a puffy white cloud equipped with a platform to stand on and a superpowered propeller underneath. The Roto-Chimp fired tiny, deadly looking missiles at Mega Man.

Mega Man ducked and ran faster. The missiles kept coming.

Mega Man ducked behind a cloud.

When the Roto-Chimp flew by, Mega Man knocked him off his Thunder Chariot and jumped aboard.

"This is the only way to go!" said Mega Man, sailing along happily through the sky. His cloud started to sink, so Mega Man switched Thunder Chariots and kept on going.

KaBooom! Mega Man whirled around to see a bomb falling very close behind him. He looked up. The bomb had been dropped by a Bomb Bird — a fat, birdlike robot flying overhead. Mega Man fired back at the Bomb Bird, but he couldn't tell if he'd gotten it or not.

Suddenly, the Thunder Chariot Mega Man was riding dived into a huge cloud. Once again, Mega Man was lost in the mists. He couldn't see a thing.

CHAPTER EIGHT

The cold, clammy mist surrounded Mega Man, closing in on him. He didn't like the feeling at all. If he had still been a robot, it probably wouldn't have bothered him. But he wasn't a robot. He was human, and he hated the way the mist got into his eyes, ears, nose, and mouth.

Most of all, though, he hated the way it blinded him. He heard creatures flying overhead, but he couldn't see anything.

That meant he couldn't aim his Metal Blade, and if he couldn't aim there was no point in firing. Mega Man couldn't wait to get out of the cloud he was in.

Finally, the mist began to thin. Soon Mega Man was back out into the blue, blue sky.

Now when the Bomb Birds attacked, Mega Man fired right back. *Blam! Kerpoww!* The Bomb Birds were destroyed, and their bombs fell harmlessly into the clouds below.

Mega Man smiled. Air Man's henchmen were no match for him!

But then his smiled faded. Mega Man gulped. Up ahead was a nasty-looking creature with quickly spinning blades set into its middle. It grinned at him as it made its blades spin faster and faster. The Fan Fiend!

Suddenly, Mega Man was knocked off his feet by hurricane-force winds. The Fan Fiend drew nearer, blowing hard.

Mega Man toppled off his Thunder Chariot and fell. Down! Down! Down! Where was he going to land?

Whump! His fall was broken as he fell right on a nearby walkway.

He ran along the walkway, dodging little clouds that seemed to be trying to trip him up. Then he saw it, parting the mists. A huge tower with a gigantic glowing W blinking on and off.

He was almost there.

Mega Man blasted through the gates that led to Air Man's inner chamber. And then he came face-to-face with his enemy.

Air Man was the scariest-looking superrobot that Mega Man had ever seen. It wasn't that he was big. It wasn't that he was strong-looking. It was his mouth.

His mouth was a huge, gaping hole that took in air and then blew it out in terrible gusts. Even though he was robot, his body seemed like it was made out of clouds. As he moved, wisps of fog evaporated off his pointed shoulders. Miniature tornadoes flew through the air, pointing their tails right at Mega Man.

Air Man stood with his back against the wall, spitting out hundreds of tornadoes. "Demolishing you will be a breeze, Mega Man!" he shouted.

Mega Man dodged the tornadoes. He tried to get closer to Air Man, but every time he approached, a tornado would knock him down and spin him around.

Mega Man gritted his teeth and kept on coming. Finally he was within range. He aimed the Metal Blade and fired. *Fwooosh! Splat!*

All the air was let out of Air Man and he collapsed like a popped balloon. The wind died down at once.

"I guess it's going to be a nice day around here, after all!" said Mega Man. He helped himself to Air Man's Air Shooter — a large cannon that fired tornados. Then he noticed Air Man's Jet-Ski — sort of a snowmobile that floated on a cushion of air — he took that, too .

Then he sat down to rest on a nearby cloud, his legs dangling over the side. "Come in, Doctor Light," he said into his radio. "Come in!"

CHAPTER NINE

For a minute, Mega Man heard only static. Then, through the crackles and pops, he heard Dr. Light.

"Congratulations, Mega Man!" the doctor said. "You really stood up against that guy."

"Oh, he was just full of hot air," said Mega Man modestly.

"Are you sure you want to go on with this mission?" asked Dr. Light.

"What kind of question is that?" yelled Mega Man. "Of course I do! Why shouldn't I?"

"Well. . . " said Dr. Light. "It just seems like each superrobot is more dangerous than the one before. And each of them has so many helpers! I'm worried about you."

"Come on, Doctor Light!" said Mega Man. "I can take care of myself." He paused. "Is there something you're not telling me?" Dr. Light cleared his throat. "Well, as a matter of fact . . . " he said. "Doctor Wily made an announcement over the news-beam this morning. He's not too happy about you destroying four of his superrobots."

"What did he say?" asked Mega Man.

"I recorded it for you," said Dr. Light. "Wait a minute and I'll play it back." There was a whirring sound, and then Mega Man heard Dr. Wily's voice.

"Mega Man!" the evil genius roared. "You little pip-squeak. How dare you even *think* about destroying me! I am invincible!" Mega Man shuddered at the sound of such villainous boasting.

"Just because you were lucky enough to get past some of my robots, don't think you'll get much further," the voice went on. "I've got some surprises for you!" Then Dr. Wily laughed. "You won't be around much longer, Mega Man. And then I'll rule the universe! Ha! Ha! Ha!"

The laughter faded out as the transmission ended.

"What do you think, Mega Man?" asked Dr. Light.

"Don't listen to that sneering bully," answered Mega Man. "I can take care of anything he throws my way. And I'll destroy him, too!"

Hearing Dr. Wily's voice hadn't really scared Mega Man at all. It had just made him even more eager to get on with his mission.

"I'm ready to take on my next enemy, Doctor Light!" he said.

"Well, all right. If you're sure about this," said the doctor. He still sounded a little worried. "Get your weapons ready. You're on your way to Crash Man's world!"

CHAPTER TEN

"So this is where Crash Man hangs out," said Mega Man, looking around. Being in this robot empire was like being inside a huge electronic machine.

There was a mazelike network of pipes rising up as far as Mega Man could see. Circuitry blinked as globe-shaped circuit breakers turned off and on. Mega Man heard beeping and buzzing as the system operated.

Mega Man tried to plan a route through the machinery. "Let's see," he said. "If I climb the ladder that runs up along that pipe there, and then jump over to —"

Just then, Mega Man was attacked by a squad of Pipe Bombers. These tiny robots looked like small sections of pipe which had broken off, grown eyes, and learned to use weapons. And there were a lot of them. They moved all around him, twirling round and round and blinking their eyes as they watched for a chance to attack him.

Mega Man pulled out his Mega Gun and fired at the small robots. *KerPOW!* Several were hit, but plenty of others took their places.

The superhero looked around wildly. The ladder he'd spotted before caught his eye, and he ran to it. Climbing fast, he outdistanced the Pipe Bombers. But when he got off the ladder, he ran right into the hideout of the Helmet Heads.

These robots were mostly helmet. They looked harmless . . . at first. Then their helmets popped up and their weapons popped out, aiming straight at Mega Man with deadly intent.

Mega Man returned their fire and kept on running. He could handle one of these guys at a time, but they kept attacking in teams.

Ahead he saw a giant circuit board. A Tronic Glider rolled around the circuit. The Glider was a platform on wheels, just the right size for Mega Man. It rode around the circuit board with no effort, as if by remote control. It didn't make a sound as it wound its way through the maze of circuitry. Mega Man leapt on just as more Pipe Bombers appeared at his heels.

The Tronic Glider carried him around the circuit. He fired as he rode, taking time to aim well. *Pow! Crash!* Pipe Bombers were falling quickly now under his fire.

Mega Man jumped off the Tronic Glider as it passed a ladder leading farther up the pipe framework. He climbed as quickly as he could. Mega Man looked up. This machine was huge! He couldn't even see the top from where he was.

Five hundred feet later, Mega Man was still

climbing. His arms were about to give out. He'd gone so high that he was once again climbing through clouds. He was reminded of Air Man's world.

Mega Man kept on climbing.

An Bomb Bird flew by, carrying a bomb. "They live here, too!" said Mega Man, ducking as the bomb fell near him.

Then he rose above the highest cloud. Now he was up in the stars.

Mega Man paused for a moment, hanging on to the ladder. It was dark all of a sudden. He had to wait for his vision to adjust.

It was a long way down. Mega Man had never been afraid of heights when he was a robot. "And I'm not really afraid now, either!" he said, as if trying to convince himself.

Still, he decided it would be a good idea not to look down.

He looked up instead, and saw an Energy Barrel on the next landing. "Perfect timing!" he said. "I can use a boost." He grabbed the barrel and drank down its contents.

A surge of energy pushed him even further up the ladder. Mega Man felt better, but he was beginning to wonder just how high he was going to have to climb.

He looked up to see if he could spot the top. Instead, he was shocked to see a Prop Top flying toward him. This was the meanest-looking robot he'd seen yet in Crash Man's kingdom.

It looked like a giant boxing glove, and it flew by means of a propeller attached to its head. And when it got close enough to Mega Man, it thrust out a long arm with a huge fist at the end of it. *Pow!*

Mega Man took a hit right on the jaw, and almost fell off the ladder. Hanging on by his fingernails, he jabbed back. The Prop Top kept advancing, and another appeared next to it.

Mega Man aimed again, carefully this time, and hit them both with one quick punch. *KaPOW-wieee!*

Grabbing a moment to look around, Mega Man saw a familiar tower with the big W. "I knew it!" he said. "These guys are guarding Crash Man. Out of my way, boys — I've got a date with your master."

He blasted past the Prop Tops and threw open the gates to Crash Man's vault.

His enemy was waiting for him. Crash Man wore a red helmet and red boots. His armor gleamed. He held a Crash Bomber in each hand, waving the weapons in the air like a cowboy at a wild West shoot-out. "Bombs away!" he called, firing at Mega Man.

Bombs flew out of the Crash Bomber and whistled through the air. They crashed to the ground next to Mega Man, exploding in a series of deafening booms.

"Those bombs are big, Crash Man, but I'm too

quick for you!" Mega Man darted around the room, firing at Crash Man with his Mega Gun. *Pow! Pow!*

Crash Man threw bomb after bomb, but Mega Man was able to dodge them all. "You think you're a superrobot, but you're nothing but a stink bomb!" Mega Man taunted.

Crash Man got angry, and he threw bombs without even aiming them. Mega Man danced around until he had a good shot at Crash Man. *Blam! BOOM!*

Crash Man was destroyed.

Mega Man marched over and picked up the Crash Bomber. He used it to hurl a bomb at the wall of the room. *BaBOOOM!* He dusted off his hands and stepped through the huge hole it had made. "Another superrobot bombs out," he said happily.

GAME HINT

Use the Metal Blade to cut right through Flash Man.

CHAPTER ELEVEN

"That was stupendous, Mega Man!" Dr. Light's voice came through the radio. "You are truly incredible. Crash Man was no match for you."

"He was all noise and no action," answered Mega Man. "And now I've got his Crash Bomber!"

"That's a very powerful weapon," said Dr. Light. "I think you'll need it, too. You'd never get through Heat Man's world without it."

"Heat Man! All right!" said Mega Man. "I'm all warmed up for him!"

"I'm keying in the password now. Are your weapons ready?" Dr. Light asked.

"Ready."

"Better get ready to use the Jet-Ski, too," warned Dr. Light. "I have a feeling you might need it."

"Okay, Doctor Light! " said Mega Man. "Wish me luck!"

Mega Man heard a faint "Good luck!" as the transmission faded out. And then, suddenly, he felt very hot.

In fact, he felt like he was about to melt. It was a new feeling for him.

Robots aren't bothered by extremes of heat and cold — their circuits adjust to any temperature they face.

But as he knew all too well by now, Mega Man wasn't a robot anymore. He was human. And he was hot.

Heat Man's world was like a giant furnace, pulsing with red-hot currents of air. Everything was the color of flame: Mega Man saw nothing but red, orange, and yellow, wherever he looked.

He reached out to touch a nearby brick wall. *SSSSzzzzzzzz!* "Wow! That's what I call hot," Mega Man said, shaking his hand and blowing on it to cool it down. "Guess I'd better keep moving."

He ran along a brick pathway, following its twists and turns. On either side of the path was a river of molten lava, boiling and bubbling as it flowed along.

"It's so hot," said Mega Man. "I sure could use a dip. But I'm not about to swim in *that* river!" He watched his step. The pathway was narrow and it would be easy to fall into the lava if he wasn't careful.

Mega Man heard something behind him and turned to see what it was.

The Prop Tops! They'd followed him all the way into Heat Man's world. He dodged their fists. If one of them hit him, the blow could knock him into the bubbling river.

"Take that!" he said, firing the Metal Blade.

ZZzzip! Powww! The Prop Tops were blasted off the pathway and fell screeching into the lava.

But there was one left. It jumped closer to Mega Man. Mega Man backed away, trying to get a clear shot at it. Moving backward, he couldn't see where he was going. Suddenly, Mega Man stumbled over a loose brick and tumbled head over heels.

"Have a nice *trip*, Mega Man," sneered the Prop Top with a wicked laugh.

Mega Man tried to catch himself, but there was nothing to grab onto.

He was falling straight into the river of hot, molten lava.

GAME HINT

To challenge Dr. Wily, you must complete all nine missions. Follow the order in this book for best results.

CHAPTER TWELVE

Mega Man couldn't believe it. If he fell into the lava it would mean certain death. Had he come this far to end up as a fried superhero, burnt to a crisp in Heat Man's world?

The lava was inches away. Mega Man could feel its heat on his skin.

Suddenly, a thought came to him. The Jet-Ski! It was his only chance.

Mega Man was wearing a special supersecret backpack designed by Dr. Light to hold all of his weapons and tools. He pushed three buttons on the special backpack control unit on his sleeve.

The tiny Jet-Ski unit popped into his hand. Mega Man could feel the lava rushing towards him. He pressed the button to unfold it, and then, not a moment too soon, he was aboard the Jet-Ski. He floated on a cushion of air, just inches above the lava river.

"That was too close for comfort!" said Mega Man, wiping his brow.

The Jet-Ski zoomed along right above the hot lava. A breeze cooled Mega Man's face as he rode. "Surf's up!" he yelled happily.

Mega Man rode for what seemed like hours. "I've just about had it with this heat," said Mega Man. "I don't know how much longer I can take it. I've got to find Heat Man and finish him off."

Just then the Jet-Ski screeched to a halt. Right in Mega Man's path was a huge, thick brick wall. "I've got to keep going," said Mega Man. "I can't let this stop me." He activated the Crash Bomber and hurled it at the wall. *KaBoooom!*

The wall was smashed into a million pieces, and Mega Man was on his way again. Just ahead, he saw a giant glowing W. He was almost there!

Mega Man blasted through the gates to Heat Man's headquarters. The ferocious superrobot awaited him, his secret weapon — Atomic Fire — at the ready. "Can you take the heat, Mega Man?"

Heat Man called. Heat Man looked like an ordinary robot, but his steel body was so hot that it glowed. The air around him sizzled. But he never felt the heat, since his protective armor kept him cool. The armor surrounded him like a huge box with a lid that could snap shut when he pulled his head inside. He looked like a square turtle.

Mega Man came on strong, jumping high to dodge the blazing fireballs that Heat Man threw. He fired rapidly, blasting away again and again. The Atomic Fire threw a whole string of fireballs at him. The flaming globes came so fast they were hard to dodge.

Mega Man's eyebrows were singed. His uniform was smoking. But he didn't give up. *Blam! BOOM! POWW!*

Finally it was over. Heat Man was just a pile of ashes. "That ought to cool your jets," said Mega Man. He picked up the Atomic Fire and signaled for Dr. Light.

"Congratulations, Mega Man!" said Dr. Light over the radio. "You really kept your cool in there."

"Heat Man wasn't such hot stuff," said Mega Man. "But I'm sure glad to be out of that furnace!"

"Doctor Wily is madder than ever," said Dr. Light. "You should have heard him on the newsbeam this time. He's furious! And he's out to get you."

"He'll be dealing with me soon enough, as soon as I get through the last two superrobot empires," said Mega Man. "It won't be long until we're face to face, and personally, I can't wait. I'm going to demolish him!"

"That's the spirit, Mega Man!" said Dr. Light. "Sounds like you're ready to take on Wood Man. Better get equipped!"

Mega Man checked his weapons as Dr. Light's voice faded out. He felt ready for anything.

CHAPTER THIRTEEN

BOOM, boom-boom, BOOM! BOOM, boom-boom, BOOM! The drums echoed through the jungle. Mega Man's blood ran cold.

Wood Man's world was like no other place Mega Man had ever been. It didn't look like the machine-filled world of Metal Man, or the broken-down buildings that were Flash Man's empire.

This was a deep, dark jungle. It was alive with a million creatures who jumped from tree to tree, going about their business. Shrieks and chatters rang from above as Mega Man tried to get his bearings.

It was hot and humid in Wood Man's world. Mega Man wiped his brow. Then he checked his weapons' energy levels, powered them up, and began to find his way through the dense undergrowth.

Suddenly, out of the bushes popped a giant, evil-looking rabbit. "What's up, Doc?" it called to Mega Man, firing its carrot-shaped missiles at the superhero.

"Robo Rabbit!" said Mega Man. Dr. Light had

told him about this not-so-funny robot. Despite its jokes and its silly rabbitlike appearance, this was a deadly enemy.

The rabbit hopped closer. As soon as it was within range, Mega Man fired the Metal Blade. "Try this on for size, you silly bunny!" he yelled as he fired.

Robo Rabbit tried to duck the whizzing blades, but Mega Man was firing too fast.

Zzzzip! Robo Rabbit toppled and fell.

Mega Man moved on, picking his path carefully. He'd only gone a few steps when he heard something above him. He looked up.

Huge black globes hung from the trees, looking like giant black apples, ready to be picked. Then, one by one, they turned into mean-looking bats that dropped onto Mega Man, flapping huge wings and making horrible noises. *Blam!* Mega Man fired as he dodged the falling bombs.

He had to move fast to avoid being blown to bits by the Bubble Bats. There were just too many of them. Mega Man was running low on energy — he didn't want to use up his precious energy pellets until he had to.

"Aha!" He spotted a tunnel ahead of him, jumped down into it, and fell. Down, down, down, deep into the earth he dropped. Finally he stopped himself by grabbing onto the root of a tree that was shaped like a ladder along the walls of the tunnel.

Should he climb up or down?

Mega Man turned and started to climb back up out of the tunnel. On his way up, he found an Energy Barrel. "Just in time!" he said, drinking it down.

He climbed for a long, long time. It seemed to take forever to find his way back to the top. Finally he saw some light up ahead.

When he came to the mouth of the tunnel, he saw why it had taken so long. He'd been climbing up the inside of a tree, and now he was high up in the treetops!

Mega Man gave a Tarzan yell. It felt so good to be out in the sun again, high above the dark jungle floor. He ran along a network of bamboo poles that made a pathway through the treetops.

Bomb Birds flew by, dropping their bombs, but they didn't slow Mega Man down. He fired at the fat birdlike robots, and dodged the falling bombs.

Mecha Monkeys popped up, hanging on to the bamboo poles. They were giant apes with more muscles than Mega Man had ever seen. They grinned at him as they held onto the bamboo with steely strength. "I hope none of these guys try to hug me," said Mega Man. "I'd be mega mush in a minute!" They waited for Mega Man to run by and tried to trip him.

"I guess it's just too dangerous up here, after all," said Mega Man. He grabbed a vine and swung back down to earth.

Mega Man looked around. There, not far ahead of him, was a giant W, blinking through the leaves. It looked like every one of Dr. Wily's evil robots had a sign over his headquarters. "Here I come, Wood Man!" yelled Mega Man as he ran through the jungle.

He was getting used to the beating of the drums. *BOOM, boom-boom, BOOM! BOOM, boom-boom, BOOM!* They were louder than ever. "What a great beat," Mega Man said. "Too bad I don't have any time to dance."

Then Mega Man saw an Atomic Chicken leaping toward him. The Atomic Chickens ran around like real chickens (with their heads cut off). They were very dangerous. If this one hit him, it would explode on contact. Mega Man wasn't about to let a chicken slow him down. He ran and jumped over it. Another one popped up, and Mega Man dodged it, too.

Finally he reached the gates of Wood Man's chamber. The superrobot lived inside a giant tree! Mega Man blasted his way inside.

Wood Man stood waiting, his Leaf Shield at the ready. "Wanna splinter, Mega Man?" he snickered. Huge green leaves surrounded him, swirling all around. Then the leaves gathered together and flew toward Mega Man. Their edges were razor-sharp. "So that's how the Leaf Shield works," thought Mega Man. He dove and was able to dodge the leaves just in time. Wood Man pounded his chest and roared. He was made entirely of wood, but that didn't keep him from yelling and carrying on like a jungle beast.

Mega Man fired back, using the Metal Blade. Wood Man ignored the flying blades. The metal weapon seemed to have no effect on him!

Mega Man switched to his Mega Gun. Leaves were flying toward him, making it hard to see. He took the best aim he could and fired.

The leaves kept coming. Wood Man was jumping all over the place, beating on his chest and bellowing loudly.

Mega Man didn't give up. He just kept on firing. *KaBLAM! Poww!* Finally, with one last bellow, Wood Man fell to the earth. The drums stopped. All was quiet in the jungle.

"You'll make a lovely footstool," said Mega Man as he took the Leaf Shield from Wood Man.

CHAPTER FOURTEEN

"Excellent, Mega Man. Excellent!" Dr. Light's voice crackled over the radio.

"Destroying Wood Man was as easy as falling off a log!" crowed Mega Man. "I wonder what Doctor Wily has to say now that I've exterminated all but one of his so-called superrobots."

"He's stayed off the news-beam," said Dr. Light. "I'll bet he's preparing for your arrival at his Castle of Evil. And I'll bet he's pretty mad, by now."

"Well, I hope he's expecting company soon," said Mega Man. "I'll be on my way to his castle as soon as I take care of Quick Man."

"Don't get overconfident now, Mega Man," warned Dr. Light. "Remember what I told you about Quick Man. He could be very dangerous."

"I know, Doctor Light. Don't worry. I'll be careful," said Mega Man.

"All right, then. Get your weapons ready!" said Dr. Light. "Password is keyed in. Give my regards to Quick Man!"

Quick Man's world was dark and quiet. Mega Man found himself in an abandoned factory, full of huge but silent machines.

The superhero walked on tiptoe. He didn't want to make any noise that might draw attention to himself. He picked his way through the enormous power plant in the center of the factory.

Mega Man kept looking around nervously. It was really just too quiet here. Was somebody — or some*thing* — sneaking up on him?

Then, up ahead, he saw an opening in the floor. An abandoned elevator shaft! "Maybe that's my way out of this nasty factory," he said, jumping down into the shaft.

The shaft was very deep. Mega Man leapt from ledge to ledge, moving down, down, down.

FWOOOOSH! A beam of light shot across the shaft. "Yikes! " said Mega Man. "Quick Man must have some kind of electric eye watching me."

FWOOOOOSH! Another one shot across, missing Mega Man by inches. "Better keep moving!" said Mega Man. "It could be a laser beam. I wouldn't want to get hit by one of those."

He continued his trip downward. *FWOOOSH! FWOOOOSH! FWOOOSH!* Beams shot past him every second now.

Mega Man decided to get out of the shaft and check his position. He squeezed through a small trap door and found himself on another floor of the same quiet factory.

It was a relief to be out of the way of those beams, but once again Mega Man felt nervous. It was so quiet!

Walking carefully, Mega Man approached a small, square box on the ground. Just as he was about to pass it, the top of the box flew open and a grinning Jack-in-the-Box jumped out. *BOOO-IIING!* It smiled at Mega Man and raised its weapon to fire.

"Yow!" said Mega Man, ducking as the Jack-in-the-Box fired at him. "That's the kind of surprise I can do without!"

He ran past the box, without even watching where he was going. And then, suddenly, he stopped short.

Right in front of him was a mean-looking robot with flames shooting out of the top of his head. He was about three feet tall, and he was wearing a tuxedo. It was Hot Head. And he didn't look like he was about to move aside for Mega Man.

GAME HINT

To kill the Wood Man, watch out for his shield and use Heat Man's Atomic Fire.

CHAPTER FIFTEEN

"Where are *you* going in such a hurry?" hissed Hot Head. "Cool your jets! Chill out!"

"I'm on my way to meet Quick Man, your boss," said Mega Man. "Out of my way!"

Hot Head didn't answer. He just nodded toward Mega Man and shot flames out of his head.

Mega Man jumped back. "So you think you're hot stuff, huh?" he asked. He fired the Metal Blade at Hot Head. *Whizz! Zzip!* The flame went out as Hot Head fell to the floor.

Mega Man stepped over the fallen robot and headed back to the elevator shaft. "I think I was safer in here!" he said, jumping back down into it.

This time the light beams started shooting very close to him. *FWOOOSH! FWOOOSH!*

Mega Man barely had time to dodge one beam before the next shot across the shaft. He knew that getting hit by one of the beams could mean certain destruction.

FWOOOSH! FWOOOSH! "That last one really came too close for comfort. How am I going to get out of here alive?" He thought for a moment. Then his eyes lit up. The Time Stopper!

He activated his secret backpack and took out

the weapon he'd gotten from Flash Man. Since he'd barely used it, the energy level still read High. *FWOOSH!* Another beam shot by, grazing Mega Man's arm. *FWOO —*

The next beam was frozen in a second. Mega Man grinned. He was safe.

Mega Man kept climbing down, activating the Time Stopper whenever he needed to. The light beams were nothing but a nuisance now.

Finally, Mega Man came to the bottom of the shaft. He popped out of the trap door and looked around. Same old factory. Same old silent machinery. It was creepy.

But Mega Man knew he had to keep going, creepy or not. He had to find Quick Man and destroy him.

He looked around. There was the giant W, right above him. Time for Quick Man!

Mega Man entered the gates. The last of eight superrobots awaited him. Quick Man stood four feet tall, but it was hard to see him. He moved so fast that he was mostly a blur. The first thing Mega Man noticed was the horns on Quick Man's head. The second was the weapon in his hand.

The horned robot aimed his infamous Quick Boomerang and threw it hard. Thousands of steel blades, whirling so fast they whistled, came closer and closer on the wings of the boomerang. "I'll have you finished off in no time, Mega Man!" Quick Man cried.

Mega Man ducked. Quick Man was fast! Mega Man fired back with his Mega Gun. Quick Man kept on coming.

Would the Metal Blade work? Mega Man aimed and fired, ducking the deadly boomerangs flying through the air. But Quick Man kept on coming.

"It's got to be the Crash Bomber," Mega Man said. "That'll take care of him." A quick press of a button on his sleeve, and the Crash Bomber was in his hand. *KaBOOOOM!* The noise echoed through the room. Mega Man launched another bomb, and another. The noise was deafening, and the room was full of smoke.

And then the noise stopped, and the smoke cleared away. Quick Man was destroyed.

"Well, I guess I slowed you down, Quick Man," said Mega Man. "Permanently!" He helped himself to the Quick Boomerang.

"And now it's on to the Castle of Evil," he said. "Watch out, Doctor Wily! Here I come!"

CHAPTER SIXTEEN

"You've done it, Mega Man!" Dr. Light's voice sang out over the radio. "It's incredible — you've destroyed every robot that Doctor Wily put in your path!"

"But my job's not over yet," Mega Man reminded the doctor. "I've got to finish off the evil genius himself. The universe is still in grave danger!"

"Yes, it's true," said Dr. Light. "Doctor Wily is still very much alive. Just this morning he flew over my laboratory in his flying saucer. He hovered there for a while, yelling through his bullhorn."

"What did he say?" asked Mega Man.

"Oh, he was threatening me," said Dr. Light. "He said I should call you off the job — or else!"

"He's probably just scared," said Mega Man. "He knows I'm on my way to his Castle of Evil. And now that he's seen me make mincemeat of his superrobots . . . "

"He seemed more angry than scared, to tell you the truth," said Dr. Light. "But I know I can't stop you now! I'll key in the password for the castle, if you're ready."

"Ready!" said Mega Man loudly.

"One more thing," said Dr. Light. "Doctor Wily has placed electronic barriers in his castle walls. Once you enter the castle, you and I will not be able to communicate. But I'll be watching you on the monitor."

"Okay, Doc!"

"Good luck Mega Man!" said Dr. Light. "Keep your wits about you and watch out for booby traps!"

As Dr. Light's voice faded out, Mega Man found himself standing alone, looking up at Dr. Wily's Castle of Evil.

The castle was terrifying . It was built of skulls and bones. The eyeholes in the skulls glowed red. Huge radar antennas were aimed in all directions. "Doctor Wily must be watching me approach his castle," said Mega Man.

He stuck out his tongue and waved his fingers in the air. "Nyahh nyahh! Here I come!" he shouted.

And then he ran toward the castle and began to climb up its outer wall.

He climbed quickly, reaching the first turret in no time. After that, the climbing was a little slower. Dr. Wily had sent out his forces. First, the Bomb Birds attacked, dropping bomb after bomb on Mega Man.

He dodged the bombs and fired at the fat little birdlike robots. *Blam!* He kept climbing.

Every time he tried to rest, another of Dr. Wily's guard robots would appear out of nowhere. They wore red armor that looked like a special uniform. Mega Man couldn't see their faces, since their helmets were equipped with shiny black face plates. They could see out, but he couldn't see in. Mega Man fought his way through them, using the Leaf Shield to hurl razor-sharp leaves, then the Air Shooter to fire deadly tornadoes.

Finally, Mega Man reached the top of the castle wall. Then he began to run. It was dark by now, but he couldn't slow down. He had to keep moving, even if it was hard to see. He raced from brick to brick.

Suddenly, Mega Man heard a train behind him.

"A *train?* What's a train doing on top of the castle?" He turned to look.

It wasn't a train. It was a dragon. A very big dragon. Breathing fire.

Mega Man leapt to a ledge and grabbed the Quick Boomerang. He aimed and fired. The dragon barely slowed down.

The immense creature began to shoot fireballs out of its mouth. Mega Man was knocked off his ledge. The dragon fired again.

Mega Man tumbled down onto a lower ledge and lay still.

The dragon came closer, to make sure that Mega Man was really finished off.

Mega Man jumped to his feet. "Surprise!" he yelled. The dragon reared up in shock.

Mega Man took careful aim and fired the Quick Boomerang again, this time right at the dragon's stomach.

The dragon fell back.

Mega Man fired again, and again. *WHUP-WHUP-WHUP!!!* The boomerangs smashed into the dragon, over and over.

Finally the fireballs stopped coming . A bright white light flashed into Mega Man's eyes. The dragon had been slain.

GAME HINT

You need to freeze time to beat Quick Man.

CHAPTER SEVENTEEN

Mega Man collapsed against a nearby brick wall. "That was a close one!" he said. "I wasn't expecting a dragon."

Nobody answered him. He longed to hear Dr. Light's voice congratulating him on a job well done. It was lonely, here in the castle.

But his radio was silent. It was time to move on.

Mega Man looked around, not sure which way to go next. The castle was gloomy and dark. The only light came from the glowing red eyeholes of a giant skull that loomed over him.

Mega Man felt like Dr. Wily was just waiting and watching. It was a creepy feeling. He decided to get going.

Right in front of him, he saw a huge iron gate that led to the inside of a tower. Mega Man decided to try opening it.

As soon as he touched it, it flew open. Mega Man stepped inside.

"*Whoooooa!*" said Mega Man, as he slid down a long, long chute.

Whump! He landed at the bottom. "Doctor Light

warned me about booby traps!" he said to himself. "Guess I'd better be more careful."

Mega Man began to walk along the dark tunnel he'd found himself in. "I must be in the basement of the castle," he said. "Guess I'll just follow my nose!"

BOOIIINNG! Just about at the same time as Mega Man said "nose," something reached out and punched him hard — right in *his* nose.

It was a Prop Top. Mega Man saw that it had its fist cocked again. He didn't feel like getting hit, so he ducked.

The Prop Top fell over when his swing met only air.

Mega Man didn't waste any time. He kept on going through the tunnel. More Prop Tops attacked him, but he didn't let them slow him down.

"Doctor Wily has called out all his forces, I guess," he said.

Suddenly he stumbled and almost fell. He caught himself by grabbing on to a ring in the wall beside him. Then he looked down.

"Just in time!" he said. There was no more floor where he'd been walking. Where the floor used to be were nasty-looking spikes lining the path through the tunnel.

Mega Man thought about turning back, but it would just mean fighting his way through the Prop Tops again. "I know!" he said. "The Jet-Ski!"

He activated his backpack and assembled the

59

ski in seconds. It worked perfectly. Mega Man zoomed along, only inches above the spikes.

Then the Jet-Ski screeched to a halt in front of a high wall. Mega Man looked the wall over. There was a tiny window in it, way up high. He rode the Jet-Ski up and looked through the window. Behind the wall was an Energy Barrel.

"I could sure use that!" he said. He activated the Crash Bomber and threw a bomb at the wall.

KaBOOOOM! The bomb exploded loudly, but the wall was still standing.

Mega Man threw three more bombs. *KaBOOOM! KaBOOOOOOOM! KaBOOOM!* Finally the wall came tumbling down.

Mega Man grabbed the Energy Barrel and drained its contents. Then he hopped back on to the Jet-Ski and kept riding through the tunnel.

Then the Jet-Ski flew through a tiny door and stopped. Mega Man got off, just as the door slammed shut behind him and sealed so that he couldn't even see where the doorway had been.

He looked around and saw that he was in a small, square room with no doors or windows. "This must be the dungeon," he said. "Doctor Wily means to make a prisoner out of me. There must be a way out, though!" He looked for an exit.

"Maybe up there, near the top," said Mega Man as he started to climb up the wall. He'd only gone a few feet when three huge bricks flew out of the walls, aimed straight at his head.

He jumped back to the floor. "More booby traps," he said. "It's not going to be so easy getting out." Bricks were flying out of the wall at top speed now, missing him by inches as he ducked and dodged. The noise was terrible as the bricks crashed against the walls of the tiny room.

"What I need now is a burst of energy," Mega Man said. He grabbed an Energy Pellet and swallowed it. Then he charged up his Metal Blade.

"Jailbreak!" yelled Mega Man, climbing up the wall. As bricks flew toward him he fired away with the Metal Blade, blowing them to bits in midair.

As he neared the top of the wall, he could see a tiny trapdoor in the ceiling. "Here's where I make my exit!" he said, squeezing through.

When he was free, he paused for a moment to catch his breath. Then he laughed out loud. "Paging Doctor Wily! " he yelled. "Paging Doctor Wily! This is Mega Man, and I'm on my way!"

GAME HINT

To get to Heat Man, use the C weapon to cut through the wall

Mega Man was closing in on Dr. Wily. "Let's see, which way now?" he asked himself.

Up ahead, he saw the castle's moat. "Maybe I'll find Doctor Wily's laboratory if I dive down and look for a secret entrance," he said.

Without a pause, he jumped in. He swam and swam.

At first, the moat seemed empty. Mega Man had thought that there might be alligators in it, but he saw nothing.

Then, just as he thought he was safe, an enormous fish swam up from below him.

They must live in the very bottom of the moat! thought Mega Man. He swam fast, trying to figure out what weapon to use against the fish, which was following him closely.

"Bubble Lead!" he cried. "Of course." He fired the heavy bubble. The fish exploded with a muffled *BaBOOOM!* Mega Man felt the waves of water wash past him. "That Bubble Lead is powerful stuff," he said. "And because it belonged to Bubble Man, it works well underwater."

Mega Man kept on swimming.

Finally, he found the secret entrance he'd been looking for.

Mega Man crashed through the door and raced through the passageway inside, using the Leaf Shield to blast his way past Dr. Wily's guards.

Still going strong, he crashed through another door and came to a screeching halt. He hadn't found the secret laboratory. He'd stumbled into Guts-Dozer's Garage.

"So this is where Doctor Wily keeps Guts-Dozer!" he said. Rolling toward him on huge steel tracks was the most gigantic robot Mega Man had ever seen. He looked like a half-giant, half-bulldozer combination. His eyes flashed with anger as he rolled toward Mega Man, waving his huge fists in the air. His orange armor glowed, and the giant spikes coming out of his shoulders looked like they had just been sharpened. Guts-Dozer was big. Guts-Dozer was mean. And Guts-Dozer was coming straight for Mega Man. He made a thunderous noise.

Mega Man felt very tiny all of a sudden. But he knew he must destroy Guts-Dozer.

He tried every weapon he had. The Air Shooter didn't even make Guts-Dozer blink. The Atomic Fire bounced off his solid steel body. The Quick Boomerang didn't even make a dent.

Guts-Dozer kept on rolling. "I'll squash you flat, Mega Man!" he roared.

He ran right over the Bubble Lead that Mega

Man threw. The Metal Blade just didn't seem powerful enough either. "The Time Stopper might buy me some time," said Mega Man, "but it won't destroy this guy. The only weapon I have left is the Crash Bomber. Let's hope it works."

Guts-Dozer was roaring even closer now. He was about to roll right over Mega Man and squash him flat. "Here I come, Mega Man!" he shouted thunderously.

Mega Man crossed his fingers and aimed the Crash Bomber. *KaBOOOOOOOOOM!*

There was a bright flash. Mega Man closed his eyes so he wouldn't be blinded. When he opened them, Guts-Dozer was gone.

Mega Man turned to leave Guts-Dozer's Garage. He could see now that it wasn't going to be so simple to get to Dr. Wily. This castle really was full of booby traps.

"If only Doctor Light could talk to me," said Mega Man out loud. " but I know he's watching. At least he knows I'm still alive."

Mega Man felt stronger just thinking about Dr. Light. He didn't feel so alone in the castle anymore.

It was time to start climbing up, out of the lower depths of the castle. Looking up, Mega Man spotted a series of long, long ladders leading up out of the basement.

"Here goes!" he said, beginning to climb.

He was getting good at climbing by now, but

it was still hard work. Mega Man struggled up the ladder.

He reached the top of the first ladder, and began to run along the walkway to get to the next one.

Suddenly, he heard the sound of static. Was Dr. Light trying to reach him? Mega Man knew that was impossible.

Then a loud voice spoke from every corner of the room. "Mega Man, this is Doctor Wily speaking! Do you read me?"

"Y-yes, I do!" said Mega Man.

"I have been watching you," said the voice. "You are quite a fighter. But you might as well give up now, because you won't get me!"

"You don't scare me, Doctor Wily!" said Mega Man. "And you better watch out, because I'm on my way!"

Mega Man ran along the walkway and through the nearest door. He had to find Dr. Wily. But instead of a hallway, Mega Man found himself in a small room with at least twenty doors. And every door was locked.

"Ha, ha, ha!" laughed the voice of Dr. Wily. "Good luck finding me, you little pest!"

Mega Man ignored Dr. Wily's voice. He took his Crash Bomber and threw bombs at every door in turn.

As each door was blasted down, Mega Man saw that there was nothing behind it. It was a trick! He was trapped!

At last, there was only one door left. He aimed the Crash Bomber and let a bomb fly. The door blew apart, and Mega Man stepped through it. "This might not be the right way, but it's my only chance," he said.

GAME HINT
When you see an Air Tiki, avoid his horns.

CHAPTER NINETEEN

Mega Man looked around. He was in another room now, a room with nine doors — or hatches, really — leading out of it. All of the hatches were blinking brightly.

"This must be Doctor Wily's Teleport System!" he said. "All I have to do is pick the right hatch and I'll be face-to-face with Doctor Wily himself!"

Mega Man looked at all of the hatches. "Eee-ny-meeny-miny-moe!" he counted. Then he jumped into the one he had chosen.

"Oh, no!" he yelled. "Not you again!"

Air Man stood in the center of the room, hurling tornadoes at Mega Man. Dr. Wily had created a backup clone of each robot.

But Mega Man wasn't about to be stopped. "I destroyed you once, I can destroy you again," he said.

It was a short fight. In just a few seconds, Mega Man came out of the hatch, dusting off his hands.

"I let the air out of him!" he said to himself, jumping into the next hatch.

In every hatch he tried, Mega Man found another of Dr. Wily's superrobots. It seemed that he was going to have to fight them all again, before he could meet their creator.

He canceled Crash Man.

He blew up Bubble Man. He mowed down Metal Man. He flattened Flash Man.

He wiped out Wood Man. He made Quick Man quit.

And finally, he harpooned Heat Man.

All the superrobots were history.

It was time to face Dr. Wily.

Mega Man jumped into the last hatch.

GAME HINT

Use Air Man's whirlwinds to defeat Crash Man, but watch out for his bombs.

CHAPTER TWENTY

It was pitch-black. Mega Man couldn't see his hand in front of his face. Where was Dr. Wily?

Suddenly, a giant spaceship appeared out of nowhere. It was enormous. Mega Man was startled. He had expected to see the evil doctor, but instead it looked like he was going to be battling aliens.

The spaceship fired at him with both cannons. Mega Man ducked and fired back with the Metal Blade. *Zzzzzip! Poweee!* The flying blades crashed into the ship.

Then the cannons stopped firing. The spaceship shuddered, and a bubble-shaped flying saucer lifted off from the top of it.

Mega Man stood watching, his mouth open in amazement. The top of the saucer lifted up to reveal Dr. Wily's evil face. His mouth was twisted in a mean smile. He raised his eyebrows and waved at Mega Man. "So long!" Dr. Wily cried, as the saucer flew off.

"NO!" shouted Mega Man. "I won't let you get away this time!"

He ran after the saucer, following it as it flew down into a tunnel. Soon he had lost sight of it, but he kept on running through the tunnel.

Acid dripped from the ceiling, sizzling horribly onto the floor below. It slowed Mega Man down, since he had to time his steps carefully to avoid it.

Finally he switched on the Time Stopper and the acid was frozen in mid-drip.

Mega Man speeded up again and kept on running.

Then he tumbled head over heels into a black void. Stars shone all around him. It was as if he'd been transported into outer space.

He didn't see the flying saucer anywhere. Had he lost Dr. Wily, after all this time?

And then a huge green mutant alien appeared in front of his eyes. Mega Man jumped back. The alien came closer.

Mega Man grabbed the first weapon he could lay his hands on. Bubble Lead! He shot it at the alien.

The alien kept coming.

Mega Man fired again, and again.

BLAAAM! KAPOWW!

Suddenly there was a superbright flash of light. Mega Man covered his eyes. Had he destroyed the alien? He was almost afraid to look and find out.

Slowly he took his hands off his eyes.

He was not in outer space anymore. He was in Dr. Wily's laboratory.

Dr. Wily had created a mirage to scare Mega

Man, but Mega Man had destroyed it with the Bubble Lead.

And Dr. Wily himself was on the floor by Mega Man's feet, begging for mercy.

It was over at last.

Mega Man had won.

> ### *GAME HINT*
>
> To get to Heat Man, use the C weapon to cut through the wall

"Mega Man, I thank you," said Dr. Light. "My family thanks you. The universe thanks you. You are the greatest superhero of them all!"

Mega Man had turned Dr. Wily over to Dr. Light for justice. The evil genius was still begging for mercy, but Mega Man knew that Dr. Light was planning to put him into prison for the next billion years.

"Mega Man, you did an excellent job," said Dr. Light. "But you look tired. If you were still a robot, you'd never be tired. Would you like me to try to make you back into a robot?"

"No way, Doctor Light!" said Mega Man. "I like being human. When I was a robot, I never had any feelings. While I was fighting my way through Doctor Wily's robots, I had lots of feelings: I was worried sometimes, I was lonely sometimes — sometimes I was even a little sad."

Dr. Light nodded. "But why does that make you like being human? Those aren't the greatest feelings in the world, you know."

"I know," said Mega Man. "But now I have some other feelings, and they *are* the greatest feelings in the world. I feel happy, and proud, and cared for. It's great to have feelings!" He paused for a moment.

"But, since I'm not a robot anymore, there's something else that I feel, too," he went on. " You were right. I am just a little tired. I think I need a short vacation."

Dr. Light laughed. "Of course, Mega Man, of course!" he said. "Now that you've taken care of Doctor Wily, the universe should be safe for quite a while. Have a good time."

Mega Man started walking, thinking about his home as he walked. He thought of his little village in the mountains. He thought about how beautiful it looked in the winter, when the snow fell all around. He thought about how it looked in the fall, when the leaves turned golden and red. He thought about how it looked in summer, with green everywhere he looked.

And soon, he was there. He looked down on his village from where he stood, high on a hill. It was spring, and flowers bloomed all over the hillside. Mega Man took off his helmet and threw it down. Then he ran down the hill, straight toward his comfortable little home sweet home.

Dear Reader,

I hope you liked reading *Mega Man 2*. Here is a list of some other books that I thought you might like:

The Forgotten Door
by Alexander Key

Have Space Suit, Will Travel
by Robert Heinlein

How To Eat Fried Worms
by Thomas Rockwell

I, Robot
by Isaac Asimov

My Robot Buddy
by Alfred Slote

The Phantom Tollbooth
by Norton Juster

You can find these books at your local library or bookstore. Ask your teacher or librarian for other books you might enjoy.

Best wishes,

F.X. Nine

WIN A NINTENDO® GAME BOY™ COMPACT VIDEO GAME SYSTEM!

You'll *score big* if your entry is picked in this awesome drawing! Just look what you could win:

GRAND PRIZE: | SECOND PRIZE:

10 Grand Prize winners!

A Nintendo® **GAME BOY**™ compact video game system

A cool video game carrying case

25 Second Prize winners!

Rules: Entries must be postmarked by November 5, 1990. Winners will be picked at random and notified by mail. No purchase necessary. Void where prohibited. Taxes on prizes are the responsibility of the winners and their immediate families. Employees of Scholastic Inc; its agencies, affiliates, subsidiaries; and their immediate families not eligible. For a complete list of winners, send a self-addressed, stamped envelope to Worlds of Power Giveaway, Contest Winners List, at the address provided below.

Fill in the coupon below or write the information on a 3" x 5" piece of paper and mail to: **WORLDS OF POWER GIVEAWAY**, Scholastic Inc., P.O. Box 742, 730 Broadway, New York, NY 10003. Entries must be postmarked by November 5, 1990. (Canadian residents, mail entries to: Iris Ferguson, Scholastic Inc., 123 Newkirk Road, Richmond Hill, Ontario, Canada L4C365.)

Nintendo® is a registered trademark of Nintendo of America Inc. Game Boy™ is a trademark of Nintendo of America Inc. **WORLDS OF POWER** ™ Books are not authorized, sponsored or endorsed by Nintendo of America.

Worlds of Power Giveaway

Name_____ Age_____

Street_____

City_____ State____ Zip_____

Where did you buy this Worlds of Power book?

❑ Bookstore ❑ Video Store ❑ Discount Store ❑ Book Club
❑ Book Fair ❑ Other_____(specify)   WOP190